A PALE HORSE PUBLICATION

DANGO DURANGO
The Bounty Hunter Series
Book 2
The Hunt for Zeke Scott

DAVID L. McADAMS

For information contact: info@Palehorsepublications.com
Cover Art by Michael Thomas
Cover Design by Pale Horse Publications
Published by Pale Horse Publications
September 2022
10987654321

DEDICATION:

This book is lovingly dedicated to – My wife Kaye who has been faithful to me since 1982. She is more skilled at living with a writer than I am at writing.

My mother H.G. McAdams for too many reasons to name. Thank you Mom for writing the poem that Dango read for Savannah at the end of this book.

My twin brother Wayne McAdams who inspired the name and creation of Clankie Claster, one of the meanest antagonists to ride the trail.

Prologue

Mentions to characters and events from other books in the Dango Durango Bounty Hunter series do come up from time to time in this book. However, it's not necessary to read other books in the series first to have full enjoyment of this book. It is possible to read them in any order and not feel lost or like you are missing something, other than the normal twists and turns on the trail the author takes you on in this journey with Dango. Enjoy.

Chapter One

"This is a holdup!"

Clankie Claster loved those words. Loved them. He wasn't merely infatuated with them, it was an obsession. He's thought about it a thousand times before actually saying them out loud, to somebody, during a stickup.

Just the night before, he'd prepared his lines again, "This is a holdup! This is a holdup!" He would change the way he said it, faster, slower, meaner, calmer, low-pitched, higher-pitched. Clankie had used this same exact phrase a lot, yet he was still preoccupied with them. Chanted them in his mind, even now, as he was saying them out loud again in the Lone Star Bank, to the dark haired girl behind the row of desks that were lined together to form a sort of counter.

He had repeated the saying over and over to himself, the night before, in the dark cave the gang he rode with holed up in. Zeke Scott, the leader of the outlaw gang, had told him he was crazy. The irony of it. Zeke Scott was as wild as they came, and for him to tell somebody they were loco, there must be something to it.

Clankie didn't care, he continued his fascination with the words he was responsible for saying during the bank robbery, practicing them in his mind. "This is a holdup! This is a holdup!"

And now, he was saying them for real, out loud. "This is a hold up!" He said it just like he had imagined it, just the way he'd repeated it over and over again at other places.

He finished his spill; this was the best part. He loved the way it fit, the next part with what he'd already said. "Hold your hands up high! Everybody!"

In Clankie's mind, he was admiring himself, the way the words so perfectly went together, "This is a holdup! Hold your hands up!" It was perfection.

Others may fall in love with people, but Clankie Claster had fallen in love with these words. "This is a holdup! Hold your hands up!"

Fixation. Passion. Mania.

He screamed it again, for effect, as he waved the heavy Volcanic pistol he'd killed at least a dozen with already, according to his own calculations, "This is a holdup! Hold your hands up!"

Everybody in the bank either started screaming or became too scared to scream.

Just before this...

Enthusiasm oozed from Ken Rowe as he bounced along on the side of the dusty road in Lone Creek. He was thrilled with every beat his heart made, and it was easily obvious.

Kenny, as his wife of a mere two years called him, didn't wear that permanent smile by accident.

He'd survived a bout with tuberculosis as a teenager, and then pulled through after the tragedy, out in the Guadalupe Mountains, in his early twenties.

Kenny's two babies, Charlie and Chelsea weren't old enough to understand what brought the happiness to their daddy. They felt it though; the radiance beamed when he held them, hugged them, threw them in the air and yelled like a kid himself.

That morning six long years ago, just after the stagecoach fell over the canyon edge and tumbled several times before landing suddenly, against jagged rocks and a field of cactus, he knew he was dead. Everybody else in the stage did die. Before the coach stopped spiraling down the cliff, they were lifeless. The driver, his shotgun holding gunman, the lady passenger with blonde curls and conversation of why she was heading west. Dead.

Townspeople would wonder the next morning what happened to the wagon. Not just what caused it to go over the canyon wall, but, where it had gone overnight. Before the town woke up, the entire stagecoach buggy was gone.

Gone.

The only thing left, at the site of the tragic event, were tracks in the red dirt of where the coach had tumbled out of control and jarred hard against rocks and a bed of cacti.

How Kenny Rowe was removed from the scene of the crash and transported to Doc's office was miraculous. No one would disagree. It was a testament of a will to live.

And so, here he was, the huge, lasting grin plastered on his face that wouldn't go away as he literally hopscotched his way to the Lone Star Bank, ready to deposit his and Lilly's latest crop earnings.

They'd only been married two years, but had already come to be known as that couple that demonstrated how love should be, should feel, should show. And it was shown; all the people of Lone Creek, each and every one mature enough to understand true love, would bear witness that nobody demonstrated married bliss like Kenny and Lilly Rowe.

It was, to some, at times, nauseating, but for the most part, folks welcomed their extended honeymoon, public passions, smiling, hugging, kissing, caressing, holding hands, and staring long and deep into each other's eyes; these were common happenings between Lilly and Kenny in the community. People could only imagine how these two acted when at home alone.

Kenny had it mapped out; he would deposit the harvest wages, stop by Ernie's Trading Square to pay on Lilly's layaway dress and pick up some cream corn for Charlie and Chelsea, then head back home just in time to play with them long and hard until lunch.

Leaping up to the bank entrance, he pushed the heavy door opened, expecting to be one of the first customers, since it had just opened up at nine o'clock. He was surprised by the line of patrons already forming.

The Lone Star Bank dedicated three young ladies to station themselves at the teller area and handle customers. Three lines were formed already, so Kenny hopped in the shortest one, wanting to hurry home and spend the rest of Monday morning with Lilly, Chelsea, and Charlie.

They had worked hard getting the crops in and taking them to market, so he didn't feel guilty at all for taking the whole morning to goof off and relax.

Just had to finish this bit of business first. Get in line, walk forward as the line moved, hand the cash to the lady behind the teller desk. Wouldn't be long now.

Kenny Rowe smiled largely while waiting for the line to move. It hadn't moved yet since he got in it. Smiling, he almost started whistling, but just then the heavy front door slammed open!

"This is a hold up!"

Clankie Claster's heavy Volcanic pistol, waving at the crowd, was the first thing Kenny Rowe saw when the outlaw gang stormed through the bank entrance.

Chapter Two

As his weighty pistol waved in the air, pointing in the general direction of the three lines of bank customers, Clankie took in the lay of the place. His mind constantly reeled. If he wasn't counting one through seven in his brain, it was because he was running some other mental mantra over and over. He actually had been guilty of rehearsing lines he would say in hold-ups at the same time he was counting one to seven. Always one through seven.

His mind processed the interior of the bank, just as it had the outside, before barging in with the rest of the gang and informing everybody they were being held up. The first thing that caught his attention, besides the cash till, were the bank employees.

Clankie's eyes were trained by experience to find where the money was at first. He knew there would be on-hand money and more stored and locked away in another area of the bank.

The on-hand money location was accounted for. Bank employees were observed. The row of desks lined up, as a counter, to separate customers on one side and staff on the other was seen. Three lines of clients with currency business. Three weak looking ladies behind the counter with plenty of greenbacks in front of them.

Clankie's mind kept taking in information. He barely noticed the rest of the gang he rushed in here with. He was so used to them being there.

Even though each of them had been assigned a specific role in the bank robbery, Clankie couldn't help taking in an overload of stimulating sights and sounds. The rush he was feeling was surged by adrenaline and his inherited recklessness.

Desert Joe would quickly get in position to keep an eye on the employees. Copperhead Cooper was in charge of making all the customers empty their pockets into the duster bag he brought with him. Slim One-Eye, who weighed two hundred pounds and really did have only one good eye, had cased the place and would lead Zeke directly to the safe. But of course, Clankie had already spotted where it might be too.

The Lujak twins were stationed outside the bank as lookouts, one at a front corner of the building and the other at the back. Raised in a remote mountainous area in the Canadian highlands, the twins had always tried to outdo each other when it came to cruelty. Each of them was a burdened load on the back of his horse, and both handled their repeater rifles with skill. They shared a motto, bullets through skulls.

The open spaced layout of Lone Star bank was more like the cavern, the gang used as a hideout, than any home Clankie had been in.

In here though, there was plenty enough light to conduct business. Customers could easily see the cash being counted to or from them. Bank robbers would also easily see the cash they made off with.

Clankie saw Zeke Scott, numero uno of the gang, looking toward the ceiling at the wagon wheels used to make chandeliers. This was something neither of them had witnessed ever, and Clankie knew it would strike a chord in Zeke.

The wagon wheels hung from the ceiling just high enough that a worker had to stand on a wooden ladder each morning to light the kerosene. Clankie knew they would not leave the bank today, without those wagon wheels that held the lanterns.

Clankie swiftly went from admiring wagon wheel chandeliers to the business at hand. His glance went directly from the lights, in the ceiling, to the smile on Kenny Rowe's face. "What're you smiling at smiley?"

Kenny just looked back at the outlaw, caught off guard and not immediately sure how to react.

"I asked you a question mister. What's so amusing?"

Kenny just wanted to finish his bank business and be on his way to his date with his wife and kids.

Spending the rest of the morning with Lilly, and the children Charlie and Chelsea, was a ton more important than getting in deep cotton with these nasty looking, gun-toting thieves. Kenny imagined these men were more than just thieves. He figured they were murderers too. They looked like it. Walked like it. They would prove very soon just how true his figuring was.

"What's a matter? Your horse got your tongue?" Clankie closed the space between himself and the stranger with the smile plastered on his face in the bank line. Kicking him just below the knee with one of his dusty, dark brown, hard leathered range boots, he repeated the question, "What's so funny mister?"

Kenny grunted at the blow and almost fell all the way to the floor. He was barely able to whisper an answer, "Just glad to be living sir, is all." He managed to stand upright.

Clankie Claster didn't think Kenny's response was reasonable enough, considering they were in the middle of a bank robbery.

Instead of taking the time it would take to rare back and club the stranger across the face with the butt of his Volcanic pistol, he committed an act that was a lot faster. With blazing speed, he jerked his old, heavy firearm straight in front of him and fired with a dead, cold conscious, violently, two feet away from Kenny's face.

Kenny Rowe was killed as dead as a man could be, before his widened eyes allowed his brain to register what had just happened.

Clankie coldly spouted, "I can't stand somebody smiling that dang much."

Slim One-Eye detoured from his path toward the safe, along with the head honcho Zeke, just long enough to celebrate Clankie's killing of the cheerful bank customer. One-Eye gave a calloused laugh, "He should've worn a gun instead of a smile." His gushing laugh continued in his hoarse voice.

Clankie scoffed, "Laughing's ok. It's smiling I can't stand."

Zeke Scott offered a quick nod of approval that went unnoticed to most in the bank. It hadn't been more'n a minute since Kenny Rowe went to meet his Maker at the hands of a man he'd never met before today. If Lilly, little Charles and Chelsea could trade that day for any other, they'd do it in a minute.

The old grandfather clock standing in the corner of the bank teller room had struck time for years. Ever since the clock salesman got top price by advertising it as an antique Long Case Clock from Britain. A minute went by, and one of the hands on the old clock moved. Another minute, the hand moved again.

Later, after the smoke cleared, the money was taken, and the gang that called themselves the Zulu Outlaws was miles from the bank, that old clock would chime loudly as it did at the top of each hour.

The hand would move, the clock would sound. Kenny Rowe would still be lifeless. He'd never move again. He would not make another sound. Lilly and those two young babies wouldn't live another day without thinking of him.

Slim One-Eye continued chuckling, as he got back on track, accompanying Zeke to the safe, guns drawn, nerves heightened. Clankie felt as proud as ever. The same stimulating feeling he gets every time.

Every single time.

"I reckon that feels as good as it gets!" He shouted in the air. "Woo! Who wants to go next?" Looking intently at the lines of customers. All of them hunkered with their heads down, hoping, praying not to be next.

Copperhead Cooper interrupted their worrying, "Empty your pockets! Put everything you've got in the bag!"

He waved the canvas bag, at some of those in line, and motioned for them to pass it around as each of them were relieved of their belongings.

He'd been in some banks where this part of the job brought as much as Zeke and Slim One-Eye took from the safe. Usually not, but he could hope.

"Hurry up! Put it all in there!"

Copperhead didn't care if it was a man or a woman. He insisted every one of them put something in his bag.

He knew they were in here on business, and business in a bank meant something valuable was changing hands. Greenbacks, pocket-watches, rings, necklaces, coins of different sorts, and other interesting items filled the bag.

"Take them boots off!" The customer did as demanded, and Copperhead tried them on, finding they fit to his liking. Throwing his old, worn boots at the customer, he grinned and looked at the new boots on his feet. The polished boots hadn't been owned long, and now they'd make footprints underneath the steps of Copperhead Cooper.

As the band of outlaws went about their routine of getting everything in the bank that was worth something, Kenny Rowe's body still laid in the same spot where he had fallen. Zeke Scott and his gang, didn't realize Kenny was worth more to his wife and children than the take they'd ride out with. They would have enough to buy a whole town once they emptied the Lone Star Bank today.

Clankie surveyed the crowd, his gun pointing proudly in their direction. His mind was busy, filled with colors and sounds. The bank design, customers in lines, fear on their faces, their crouching bodies, greenbacks, gold pocket-watches, outlaw gang members, recent recollections of his finger pressing the trigger and his eyes watching the smiling stranger fall dead, one thru seven. As the colors, sounds, and recent memory raced through his brain, he continued counting one, two, three, four, five, six, seven, one two, three, four, five, six, seven…

Chapter Three

Fascinating things were happening in Lone Creek. More intriguing than a passerby would take in while, just sitting at the stage coach depot, waiting for the next ride out during a layover. Just the happenings in the Lone Star Bank this very minute could prove the remarkable complexities.

The name Zeke Scott had become one that struck terror in folks when they heard it. If he was actually near, the alarm intensified immensely. That penetrating fear was occurring inside the Lone Star Bank, and Zeke hadn't fired a shot. Up to now, Clankie Claster was the one bringing all the badness to the bank.

The outlaw gang had formed just as a major event in America was winding down. The event and the forming of the gang were both incredible to say the least. Each had life and death stakes, and both believed in their causes.

Zeke had several aliases, including Zeke Zulu Scott, ZZ Scott, and just plain Zeke Scott. His ma and pa had named him Ezekiel Obadiah Scott. The gang he was becoming commonly known to be boss of was notably called the Zulu Outlaws. They were made up of several different cultures.

Desert Joe was self-acclaimed to come from the Navajo bloodline.

Slim One-Eye swore there'd never been anyone in his family tree that wasn't white.

Clankie Claster wasn't right sure of his heritage. He guessed it to be part Caucasian and the other part Mexican from the old country. One thing he did know; everybody he was kin to was filled with impure meanness. The Lujak twins believed themselves to be mostly Canadian with a streak of French in their veins.

The remaining two members of the Zulu Outlaws was Copperhead Cooper and the boss himself, Zeke Scott. Both men had memories of slavery. Real memories. Personal memories. They had each been the possession of other men. Both utterly insisted that since they'd tasted freedom, they would never be anybody's slave again. Never!

Zeke and Copperhead had deeply ingrained convictions that they would kill or be killed before ever being enslaved or imprisoned. So far, they had killed several to keep those convictions alive. The madness of it, claiming to own a man just because of his color. This was at the heart of those convictions, and an unstoppable drive kept those beliefs strong.

Reaching the safe, Copperhead slung the man in the best suit in the place, the one he suspected to be the bank president, toward the safe in the corner.

"Open it!"

The bank president, Mr. Hagley fell hard against the iron safe, staggered to upright himself and went as quickly as he could to the chore of getting it open. He knew there were thousands behind that locked door. His own convictions yelled at him to not open it.

He sensed that he would be as dead as that smiling stranger in the teller line, screamed at him that he better open it as fast as he could, and let the two dark outlaws in the safe room with him have whatever they wanted from it. His heart was beating as fast as his thoughts were running.

Fumbling fingers seemed to be fooling with the safe instead of taking it serious.

"You've got less than ten seconds to get that blasted thing open! If not, you'll be dead and we'll get it open ourself!"

That did more to shake Mr. Hagley's nerves than to calm him. He wasn't about to try and correct their grammar. The fumbling worsened. Somehow, in spite of his nerves and his racing heart, and his fearful anxieties, and the shadow of the two foreboding bank robbers, he managed to cause the safe door to fly open on its hinges.

Copperhead shoved him out of the way and reached for the pile of greenbacks instantly. Zeke pointed his Colt Army Model at Mr. Hagley, intending to use it for more than just keeping him from stopping them.

He had taken the forty-four caliber military revolver from the man who condescendingly called himself his slave master. Zeke remembered the very day he had stolen the muzzle loaded revolver. It was just after he'd strung the man up inside the old barn.

Chicken hawks were the first to find the slave owner hanging in the outbuilding. Then, buzzards showed up and chased them away from the swinging carcass.

There were things he didn't like about the Colt, but he especially appreciated the way it looked. That was important to him, the way things looked. And right now it looked like he would use that revolver again to take another important man's life.

Zeke was bothered more by the importance of a man than by his skin color. Certainly, since his former owner had been white, he had challenges dealing with those of that color. But the main problem he had was when people thought they were better than others.

He allowed several men to ride with him of various colors and ethnicities, but these men didn't think they were better than others. They knew it. And they had the same proving grounds that Zeke Scott struggled with. Even though they'd never been enslaved because of their colors, they had each been looked down on for one reason or another.

The hatred that had become entrenched in them was pouring out now in the Lone Star Bank of Lone Creek. Zeke Scott pulled the trigger once. The lead ball shot

from the barrel of his Colt Army Model and pointlessly took the life of the bank president, Mr. Hagley.

Two lives had been needlessly snuffed out inside the bank, but thousands in legal tender had been taken. When the gang rushed out of the bank, just as hard and sudden as they had entered, customers and employees didn't feel like they could breathe sighs of relief. They were anxious because two men had been murdered. They had been stripped of valuables. They weren't convinced the outlaw gang wouldn't return and finish off them all.

Dust swirled in the street as the Zulu Outlaws slapped at their horses, speeding away from the bank. It had seemed like an eternity to those who were still in the bank. The time had flown by for the outlaws. They would be back at Claster's Cavern, counting the loot, before those back at the bank exhaled.

Chapter Four

Five years had passed since the Emancipation Proclamation was delivered by President Lincoln. He had been killed just a couple years after that proclamation, and his Vice President, Andrew Johnson took over the top spot in the country.

Andrew Johnson's presidency began just as the Civil War was ending and right in the middle of Zeke Scott's reign of terror. The war had heightened people's sense of awareness and caused many warm natured folks to grow cold.

The excellent giftings and qualities of numerous darker skin citizens were finally allowed by the nation to be revealed. One such man was the Lone Creek Sheriff, CW Lee. He was elected sheriff of the area as soon as it was possible, given the divide in opinions of the times.

Times were still not perfect; some days the job as sheriff was still very difficult. After all, he was a lawman in a region that only recently begun seeing CW and his family as people, instead of property.

Times in Lone Creek had been anything but calm since CW took office. Calm couldn't be expected for an area that had just gone through war, had just witnessed slaves becoming free, had just personally experienced one of those former slaves being installed as the sheriff of the entire county.

When folks asked about Lone Creek, they were quickly informed that Lone Creek was the city itself, and that the entire county was also called Lone Creek.

CW Lee's sheriff office sat in a building that doubled as courthouse and jail for the county. Little did he know this area would soon be the epicenter for the manhunt for Zeke Zulu Scott.

Chapter Five

Sweat poured down his dark, leathery skin. The shirt worn by the man, pounding the anvil in the blackness of a deserted cave entrance, seemed more like a perspiration soaked, light tan colored loincloth instead of a shirt. More flesh was exposed of his back and chest than not. He liked it that way, allowed the breeze to flow and cool him somewhat.

Claster Cave used to be the entrance to old man Claster's mining outfit. The operation had existed until they hit a long dry spell, and then moved to another town to try their quarrying efforts.

The old geezer, known as Mr. Claster to his mining employees, did not actually have any prior mining experience. He simply had an entrepreneur's mind and saw this as an opportunity to make a fast load of denaro.

This wasn't the first mine to be abandoned by the Claster clan, nor it wouldn't be the last. It made for the perfect place for an outlaw gang to hole up.

When old Mr. Claster left, his only son Clankie stayed behind with the abandoned mine, figuring joining with an outlaw gang would be more profitable and more exciting.

Zeke hammered away; aware the sounds of his tool striking the hot metal on the anvil would echo and bounce off nearby mountains.

He knew there wasn't a soul for miles and had no hesitations about all the racket he was making.

The bank loot had been divvied up proportionately. Clankie, Copperhead Cooper, the Lujak twins, Desert Joe, and Slim One-Eye had each taken equal portions, while Zeke kept fifty percent of the entire take for himself. None of the men argued with him about it or even showed displeasure with it. He thought it was fair and would shoot anybody who tried to convince him otherwise. They knew it, and he knew it.

He went on with his hammering, thinking this could turn out to be more profitable than the bank robbery business. A thought occurred to him, Ol' Mr. Hagley wouldn't argue it with me either.

Clankie Claster strolled up from deeper in the cave. As he was about to ask the boss if there was any way he could help, his mind was strumming, one, two, three, four, five, six, seven…

Chapter Six

Dango Durango headed west through the mountains of Colorado. After his recent near death venture and fight to regain his strength, he was back to his old self. He felt stronger now than he did before the tragic few months he'd spent just this side of the edge of demise.

Leaving Savannah back at the Briar Patch was harder for him than chasing a bounty. He couldn't get away from it though. The hunt was in his blood.

He was thankful to his ol' friend Weed for stepping up and riding with him again on the chase they had made for Gus the Pawnee. There were countless memories of riding with Tumbleweed. Dango just called him Weed for short, and they'd spent many a day and night in each other's company.

Campfires, gunfights, brawls with fugitives, good times, bad times, better times, worse times; Dango and Weed had experienced working as sheriff and deputy, riding with a posse, riding alone just the two of them; they had gone through a lot together. Some of those days and nights had seemed like Heaven; some had seemed a whole lot like visiting hell itself.

Many memories of Dango and Weed riding together flooded his mind as he rode west, heading to Cactus Junction. He just had to go see his old friend and personally give him the latest news.

Dango remembered the night Weed had turned to him, over a campfire, and spilled his heart to him. The dreams he had of having his own cattle ranch, a wife and kids. He'd set out on that journey, and now he owned the largest ranch in this part of the state.

However, ol' Weed was still waiting for the rest of the dream to transpire. He still hadn't met Mrs. Weed, nor had he started having any of his own children.

Dango couldn't wait to reach Cactus Junction. He hoped this news would encourage Weed. He definitely didn't want to dishearten his old partner on the right side of the law, but he had enough sense to know there was a chance of that. He rode on, looking forward to seeing his old bounty hunting running buddy again.

Chapter Seven

It was a long, hard ride, but Dango finally arrived at Cactus Junction. Two of Weed's gunhands were situated up front on the road leading in to the Circle-W ranch as sentries. Others were patrolling in the woodline on the ride up to the ranch. It had been known that someone was approaching long before he got to the wide, gated entrance.

The heavy, wooden gate swung open from east to west as one of the lookouts pushed hard on it. "Dango, it's good to see you again. How you been?"

"Mighty fine my friend."

The smile on Dango's face showed he meant what he'd just said.

"The boss man will shor' be glad to see you again."

"I'm sure of it. Hasn't been that long this time, has it?

The gunhand chuckled, remembering just a few months ago when Dango had ridden up, after more than a couple of years, and got Weed to ride with him again.

Magnificent canyons and high, red buttes filled the horizon to the west. North of the ranch, mountains covered in pine trees seemed to reach the sky. To the northeast, green, lush, grassy plains and valleys stretched for miles between the mountain ranges.

Weed had picked the picture-perfect place for his compound. The ranch had several structures he and his men had built with their own hands. He had his own home place made out of barked logs and clapboard siding. The ranch hands lived in the bunkhouse that was spacious enough for comfort for more than fifty of 'em.

The building in the middle of the fenced off area was the operations center. Weed and his workers called this the headquarters. It was also built out of logs and clapboard siding, but they used stone as well on this command center. It really wasn't as modernly developed as it sounded, but they liked using those terms for the place where Weed's ranch office was.

This whole part of the ranch, the bunkhouse, Weed's home, headquarters, corrals, pastures, a two-story barn, and stables, were all fenced off with a fence made from birch trees, as far as you could see.

Dango rode through the gate at the entrance to the Circle-W and headed to the ranch office. Twilight knew the way and instinctively trotted briskly in that direction.

Reaching headquarters, Twilight slowed to a stop without so much as a whoa boy from Dango. It wasn't necessary. They'd ridden in here plenty of times since Weed built this place from the ground up.

One of the several workers roaming the compound shook hands with Dango and gave Twilight a rub on his forehead.

"I can get this old boy over to the livery stable for ya if ya want."

Dango stroked Twilight on the slope of his nose just below his eyes, "I'll see you in a bit boy. Go get some grub and some rest."

"It's good to see ya again Mr. Dango."

"Same here. Thanks for offering to see to Twilight for me."

The ranch hand led Twilight towards the stables as Dango walked inside the massive building known as headquarters. As soon as he stepped inside, his old friend spotted him. "Well, if it isn't Dango Durango."

They quickly covered the main room of the building and greeted one another, slapping shoulders and beaming with wide, teeth-showing grins.

"What in the world brings you way out here so soon? Hasn't been much more'n a few months since we chased that Injun."

Dango laughed lightly at the reference. "I still owe you big time for that one."

"What are you talking about? I know you'd drop everything at the drop of a hat, for me, too. Matter of fact you've already done that several times."

"Well, don't worry, this ain't no business call." They both snickered. "I rode over here to see to it that you heard it from me."

"What's that Dango?"

"You remember Savannah?" He realized what he'd just said. "Well of course you do. I've asked her to marry me."

Weed's lips curled upward as far as they could without making him look silly. "Man, Dango, that's great." He paused and added, "Did she say yes?"

The laughing began between both men. "Of course she did Weed. You think I'd ride all the way over here with this news if she'd said no?"

"Wouldn't be the first time you'd come and seen me with a heartbreak."

Dango laughed out loud, realizing that was surely true. "Well this ain't no heartbreak this time. I want you to be my best man at the wedding."

"Best man? What in the world does a best man do?"

"I figure you'll just stand at the front with me and stand guard in case anybody wants to try and keep this marriage from happening. I won't be wearing my gun during the ceremony, but you can be armed and ready. It's called best man, and you're the best with a gun that I know."

The laughter continued, "You know ain't nobody gonna try and keep that marriage from happening. Besides that, ol' Jake Starnhall would give me a run for my money as far as being best with a firearm."

Weed insisted his old friend stay til morning. It was festive at the Circle-W that evening with plenty to eat and drink. Lively music played late into the night with conversation continuing the same way it had begun when they were discussing the wedding.

Chapter Eight

The next morning, Weed's chuckwagon cook, Turnip, fixed the tastiest vittles a soul could have for breakfast. Pricilla served hotcakes with honey, eggs, bacon, grits and gravy. She had lived and worked at Weed's home place, since the day some of his men found her, lost near the towering red buttes west of the compound.

Pricilla, young and dark-skinned, had been separated from her family after they came from the Yucatan. They made it through some rugged territories of Mexico and Colorado before bandits took her ma and pa and her little sister.

She was desperate when Weed's men found her. Since that day, she hadn't heard from her family. At twenty-four, she was finally beginning to think of this place as home and Weed and his employees as her family.

She managed to keep her attitude as shiny as her long, black hair. She looked several years younger, than her age, in spite of the hard years she'd known. Her conversational English was understandable, but heavily accented.

Turnip, on the other hand, looked every bit as old as he was. He'd ridden many a trail and cooked in the same pot for years over a danged lot of campfires.

He fared well at keeping his cloud-colored white hair trimmed short and kept a week old bristle of a moustache and beard. His round body showed that he relished eating what he cooked. And he actually liked cooking about as much as he delighted in eating.

Finishing the hearty breakfast, Dango mentioned two things to Weed, one very serious and the other very light-hearted.

Pulling out a tattered wanted flyer, Dango reported, "I gotta go ol' friend. This here's a fellar called Zeke Scott, been killing folks and taking things that don't belong to him. I'm heading down Texas way to find him and bring him in."

"You need some help, you just give me a holler."

"You know I will Weed. I don't foresee having to do that this time though."

Before Weed could respond, "Another thing I was noticing. That girl Pricilla, I think you two could really have a good thing going together."

Weed looked at Dango like this wasn't something he hadn't already had cross his mind. "You're a keen observer. We've just recently started realizing these kinds of feelings between the two of us. We've just barely had time to start exploring those very notions."

Dango smiled at the way Weed was trying to express what he knew to mean that he and Pricilla had just started romancing each other.

And it was too new to have out in the open for everybody to gawk over. He felt assured now,

knowing this, that his great news of the upcoming wedding wouldn't depress his old friend Weed.

"Perhaps next time we see each other, you'll be asking me to be your best man."

Weed smiled at the thought, and Dango began to laugh. The laughter grew louder when they noticed Pricilla had come back in the room and heard the last part of their conversation.

All three of them had good feelings gushing through them, and not long after that Dango headed out the door, Texas bound.

Chapter Nine

"Those hellacious cads have it coming to 'em! Every detestable one of 'em!"

The air in the shadowy cave was hot, not from the temperatures, as it was fifty-eight degrees back this far in the hollow.

Zeke Scott and his band of outlaws were a couple of rooms back. Claster's Cavern consisted of several connected areas. They called the entrance Claster Cave. This front part of the caverns was a large expanse where enough sunlight emitted in, to allow moving about and even working on gang projects with a few more extra light sources. If they wanted to meet up in the entry to the caverns, they simply referred to it as Claster Cave.

The caverns were comprised of what they called rooms. Actually, they were quite a few caves linked together. Some of the rooms or caves were somewhat large; others were so small that most of the men had to duck to walk through them.

Just enough oil lamps were burning to let the gang members see each other as their ranting meeting continued. The air in this cave was heated and getting hotter as the head of the Zulu Outlaws spouted his propaganda. It didn't seem like hoopla though, and it wasn't received in here that way either. He was preaching to his choir.

"We won't stop until every lousy one of 'em is dead! We won't be stopped until they're all buried!"

Copperhead Cooper, Slim One-Eye, Desert Joe, the Lujak twins, and Clankie Claster listened intently as Zeke shouted his agenda in the dim cave. As soon as he took a breath, they would shout back at him like a congregation yelling amen to a preacher. Then, he'd start right back at spitting his agitating messages.

By the time they'd been at it almost an hour, they were more stirred to hatred than ever. That disgust would be followed up with action. The time spent in the cave, riotously rousing each other, did not tire them at all. In fact, it did just the opposite. They were so fired up and energized for finding and bringing agony to those who represented Zeke's former slave owner that they'd be out of Claster's Caverns that very day to carry out their plan.

Chapter Ten

The gang was an oddity for their era. Two of the outlaws were dark skinned, or as some people of the times called them, colored. One was Navajo Indian through and through, and one was a pure pale face, or the term some used for his kind, white. Another gang member was part white and part Mexican. The two twins were Canadian and French.

So the gang, even though there were two coloreds, one white, another white and part Mexican, two Canadians with part French, and an Indian, they were united in their mission. Each knew the role he would play today, and each would carry out their respective parts believing the gang's endeavors wouldn't be carried out properly without him.

"Twins, set up on that ridge." Zeke never called the Lujak brothers by name, figuring that way he'd never call the wrong one by the wrong name.

They each pulled slightly left on the reins and guided their paint horses to the left. That ridge west of where they split off from the rest of the gang, would be a perfect lookout.

How the twins had come across and claimed the two white horses, with similar brown makings, was a treasured memory to the gang.

They were a testament of how far the gang would go to evade capture and the dark depths of hell they would

travel to, so they could avoid the light that glistened off a sheriff's star.

They could tell with vivid mental imagery and colorful words of how two volunteer posse members strayed away from the rest of the group and traded their lives to the Zulu Outlaws in exchange for the Lujak twins taking ownership of the beautifully painted steeds. Each horse stood about 16 hands high and made the transition from law work to outlaw work fairly well.

"The rest of you follow me."

Zeke spurred his stocky dun Barb horse, and he started a quick gallop to the east, heading for the edge of a tree line not far from the dusty roadway.

The horse Zeke owned had come from when he hung his slave master in the two-story barn behind the main house. His owner had traded for it with Indians, who had received it in a skirmish with Spanish Conquistadors, who forgot to go back to their homeland, after exploration in this part of the world.

The Barb horses had been used by the Moors during an invasion of Spain because of their barbaric ways. This breed was by nature barbarous, ferocious, cruel, brutal, anything but gentle. This fit perfectly with Zeke Scott.

Reaching the tree line, "Y'all stay put. I'll head to the bend back up the road and watch for the stage. When I see it coming, I'll head back this way and hide in that cactus bed."

As soon as I leave that bed of cactus and head to the road, y'all come charging as hard as you can. We'll surround 'em with surprise and guns blasting. They won't know what hit 'em until it's too late."

The bed of cactus Zeke referred to wouldn't conceal the whole gang, but it would be enough cover for just him and his vicious dun Barb horse.

Zeke goaded the dun and he turned on his horseshoes, sprinting back towards the bend in the path. When they got to the turn in the road, he pulled the reins to bring the horse, he proudly named Ghengis to a halt.

They veered just to the edge of the trail, and Zeke pulled his telescopic spyglass from the saddlebag and peered up the dry, dirt road watching for the stagecoach to come heading that way.

Slim One-Eye had cased the place for at least a week, so Zeke knew it wouldn't be long before the stage line headed this way on its route to Lone Creek.

He didn't wait more than a half hour until he saw the dust coming up from the horse hooves and coach wheels. Less than a moment later, he saw the outline of the horses and stagecoach buggy itself.

He knew from One-Eye's updates, there'd be Ben West the driver, Sam Harker the shotgun rider, and who knows how many passengers. Ben and Sam would both be heavily armed as they carried the payroll for the state penitentiary.

Slapping Ghengis with his spurs, they rushed back up the trail heading for the bed of cactus. The men in the tree line knew what was about to happen and became more alert. The Lujak twins held their position, watching all directions, making sure they wouldn't be surprised by anything or anybody.

The stage rounded the curve in the road, dust following. Ben West, Sam Harker, and the lone stagecoach passenger weren't mindful about what was waiting for them up the way.

Chapter Eleven

As the stage approached, going at a steady pace, Zeke and Ghengis rushed from behind the wildly growing scrubs of cactus. The rest of the men who had been hiding in the dense tree line moved out at his cue. The Lujak twins stayed put on the western ridge, just in case.

With guns firing in the air, the men encased the stagecoach, daring it to keep going. Sam Harker died at the onset of the robbery, with a daring, impossible move.

As Zeke Zulu Scott, Desert Joe, Copperhead Cooper, Clankie Claster, and Slim One-Eye circled the stagecoach with guns drawn and already shooting, Sam had reached for his side by side, double barrel, twelve-gauge shotgun and raised it to press the first trigger on the powerful weapon.

He got the initial shot off which spiraled wildly into the air. Before he could get his finger on the second trigger for the next barrel, he was struck in the forehead just over his left eye. None of the gang actually knew whose gun the shot came from, but they'd all take the credit for killing such a daring and crafty shotgun rider.

Ben West strained hard to bring the coach to a stop. The four horses were tiring from a long run and were easily spooked by the piercing gunshot sounds.

He had them slowed and was making progress,

but when Sam's double barrel had boomed, not far from their ears, they'd picked up frenzied speed, and Ben thought for sure he'd be killed too before they came to a dust spewing stop.

"Come on down from there!" Zeke didn't wait a second before shouting demands.

Ben West jumped from his seat up front of the coach and landed like a young man on the hard, sandy surface. Normally, it would take him a few minutes now days to climb down.

He had driven for the Wells Fargo line, between Nebraska and California, before heading down south and hiring on with this outfit.

He wasn't as young as he used to be, and his body reminded him of it every time he hopped down from his rider's perch on the stagecoach. He would certainly feel it tomorrow after leaping down so recklessly. That is if he lived until tomorrow. Seeing his shotgun rider slumped dead in the seat, he had his doubts.

"Hurry it up!" Zeke was hopped up on adrenaline as was the rest of the gang.

As Ben reached the ground and up-righted himself after the hard landing, he naturally put both hands in the air. Both of his weapons had been left in the driver's seat, the rifle and sidearm. He had felt pretty helpless even while they were in his possession. He really had an abandoned feeling now.

About half the men ganged up on old Ben while the other half banged the passenger door around until they got it open and the lone passenger thrown out on the ground.

The passenger had an appearance that would allow every criminal of the Zulu Outlaws to pick him out as a professional gambler. His long, dark duster coat reached just above his knees. He wore a dark derby hat to match. The dark clothes gave the impression of someone who was serious minded. Someone who would consider all the possibilities before showing his hand.

His colorful, red puff tie showed he was serious about being flashy and flamboyant. Even the frilly ends of the sleeves on his white dress shirt stuck out the end of his dark duster sleeves. This all combined with his dark, pleated pants and polished shoes to substantiate that he worked at maintaining a particular look.

The Lujak twins held to their post on top of the ridge as Zeke and the others rummaged through the coach. Both the driver and passenger were searched and emptied of everything they had on them.

The driver didn't have much besides his two firearms. The passenger was relieved of two decks of cards and about a thousand in United States Notes.

These greenbacks wouldn't see a poker table any time soon, but they would be distributed among the gang later back at the hideout. Zeke would get his customary fifty percent while the rest of the men would split what was left.

A bigger payday for them to share came from the Colorado State Prison payroll. Copperhead Cooper almost squealed when he opened the box, "There's at least twenty thousand in here!"

The men celebrated by whooping and hollering. New gunshots rang out loudly. All of the gang, except Zeke and the Lujak twins, reacted by jumping quickly on top of the horses attached to the stagecoach. The horses had been startled by the deafening bangs. The men fought and jerked the reins to keep them from racing off with fright. They surely didn't need the horses running off with the currency and leaving them standing there without it.

The Lujak twins watched from their elevated spot, as the gang worked to finish the hold-up, once they got the horses under control. They worked with precision, and it didn't take long until they were satisfied with what they'd done and headed out.

As they charged down the sandy path, the Lujaks fell in behind them. Before they picked up much speed on the trail, Slim One-Eye hollered and asked Desert Joe, "Do you think we ended the best way possible back there?"

Desert Joe whimsically answered, "I think it's hilarious. Just wait til somebody finds 'em like that."

Chapter Twelve

It had been more than a week since Dango boarded a train to head south to Texas. Traveling the mountain pass in Colorado at over ten thousand feet elevation with sheer drop-offs, sharp curves, and quick inclines and declines made for a precarious trip. He enjoyed the views; though realizing the dangers of such steep grades on the rail line helped his prayer life.

Dango was pleased that Twilight didn't have a direct outside view from the stock railcar. He wasn't really sure if the perilous gradients on the slick rails would bother him or not. He had always seemed sure footed when riding through any type of country.

They had unloaded from the train a day's ride away from Lone Creek by stage. After the long stagecoach ride, they finally arrived to their destination.

After the rugged journey, Twilight had spent that first night in Lone Creek in the coziest bedding he'd laid in for a while. Dango slept very well at the only lodging house in town.

The next day, he had a scrumptious breakfast at the Stone family restaurant. Harold and Lois had relocated in Lone Creek from farther south, and folks took a quick liking to them. Especially once they tasted the comfort foods they offered.

Lone Creek citizens couldn't get enough, and the place was crowded three meals a day, seven days a week.

Before the Stone family opened their place, people didn't really have any public eating place available. It was commonplace for someone to ask how they could get meals they made at home to taste so different and so good at their restaurant.

Dango had already discovered that. He thought to himself, 'This is enough reason to move to Lone Creek, for the fine eating at this place.' Although he knew chances were slim, he'd actually ever settle down here. He had thought about Savannah every day and night since leaving Colorado.

After the early morning feast, he had gone over to the livery stable and found Twilight looking happy as could be. The two of them had spent the better part of the day ambling the outskirts of town trying to catch the trail of Zeke Scott.

Later in the day, they had ridden over to the jail, arriving there a few hours before sundown. Dango found Sheriff CW Lee inside the jailhouse.

When Dango walked in, the sheriff was grabbing a rifle from the gun case. He pushed the door shut on the case and pointed the rifle to the floor before turning to see the stranger come in the door of the jail.

"What can I do for you sir?"

Dango saw the tin star first, after seeing the rifle that is. The next thing he noticed was that the sheriff was not a white man.

He was about five-fee- ten inches with a stocky build. Even though he had a barrel chest, his gut

was about as large from all the biscuits, gravy, vegetables, and meat Mrs. Lee had so capably prepared over the years.

The dark man wore denim trousers, a solid color long sleeve, cotton, button up shirt, and a thin, brown cowhide vest with the star pinned to it. He had a thick southern twang in his accent.

Dango greeted the sheriff in his deep voice, "Howdy Sheriff, my name's Dango Durango."

The two shook hands. CW seemed distracted, like something was weighing on his mind, "Pleased to meet you sir, CW Lee. I'm the sheriff in these parts."

"I reckoned that from the star." Dango regarded the star pinned to CW's vest as he glanced at it.

"You reckoned right. Don't likely think we've met."

"Probably not Sheriff. I came in yesterday evening, on the stage, after a long ride on the rail from Colorado."

CW's words came slowly, "Mercy, that is a long trip. You must have some awful important business to travel all this way by rail and coach."

"Well actually that's why I stopped in here. I'm a bounty hunter, and I got word Zeke Scott is running in this neck of the woods."

"You don't say. That could shorely explain a whole lot."

"How's that sir?"

"Just call me CW. We've been having a lot of unexplained violence going on in these parts.

Lots of thangs missing. The bank was robbed and cleared out a little over a week ago. A young family man, Kenny Rowe, and Mr. Hagley, the bank president, were found dead."

"You think it could've been Zeke Scott?"

"Hard to say. The strangest thang; everybody at the bank, when we showed up, was out of their mind loco. They were disoriented and didn't remember anythang that had happened thar. Two dead men and the bank robbed of every paper note it had. And not a one of them could tell me anythang about what had gone on in thar."

"That's mighty peculiar. Don't think I've ever heard of anything like that before."

"Me either Mr. Dango. We gotta wrap this up. I was just heading out to check on the stage. It should've been here hours ago. Now that you've told me Zeke Scott might be in this area, you've really got me wondering."

"Mind if I ride out with you CW."

"Shore thang."

Heading out front, the two lawmen saddled up and headed out, wondering what they'd find on the stage route into Lone Creek.

Chapter Thirteen

Dango had enjoyed the beautiful Texas views on the ride out of town with the sheriff. Everyplace he'd been recently in his travels brought its own scenic sights. He had to admit he had been blessed on this trip by seeing some of the most stunning places he'd ever witnessed.

He could tell of seeing mountains in Colorado and New Mexico that are probably the subject of paintings in a gallery somewhere. Here in this part of Texas, one thing that strikes him is the vast amount of towering, pine trees that he's told stays green year round.

The pine boughs on these trees are springy branches with straight pine needles and black pine cones. The trees have tap roots that sink deep into the ground, allowing them to be hearty and withstand Texas tornados. CW said he'd seen the tops of the pines in this area bend to the ground during a storm and stand back upright when the wind quit blowing.

Dango was taking in all of it. Not only was he feeling a sense of satisfaction from the splendor of seeing God's creation; he actually smelled the strong fragrance of the pine needles with a gentle breeze blowing through them.

Pine has a unique smell, and he breathed in the Texas air deeply, the scent not overwhelming, but enjoyable.

He was amused at how the greenery seemed to quickly change and the countryside started to dry out the farther out of town they got. He was beginning to see less dark and bright green and more dry browns and light greens.

"There's something up ahead," CW mentioned as soon as he spotted it.

Dango's enjoyment of all the sights and smells quickly took a hard turn. He saw two men wandering lively in the middle of the dirt roadway.

He noticed a man lying partially on his side and partly on his belly, on the ground.

Jumping down from Twilight, he sprinted to the one who was lying on the ground. As soon as he rolled him over, he noticed the dried blood on his forehead, where the bullet had entered.

Sheriff CW trudged up quickly behind him, "That's Sam Harker, one of the best shotgun riders I've met."

"He's dead Sheriff."

"Let's check on these other men. They look like they've gone out of their mind."

Dango looked at the other two men circling in the road, stirring up dust. They were talking incoherently, laughing hysterically one minute, and seeming to be scared out of their wits the next.

As the sheriff and Dango approached the men, one of the characters fell flat and began beating his fists on the hard clay, that had been packed by the stagecoach

that routinely came through this way.

He was giggling like a schoolgirl whose boyfriend had just discovered her funny bone.

The other feller charged as fast as he could from the road, and fell to a hiding spot behind a six-foot Saguaro cactus, scraping against some of the spiny needles on the way down. He appeared to be fearing for his life like someone or something very heartless was about to get him. His eyes were bewildered.

The area was littered with prickly pear and barrel cactus, besides the many upright Saguaro cactus.

CW immediately recognized the gentleman who was laying on the ground cackling. "Ben! Pull it together! Ben! What in the world's going on with you?"

Dango had gone to the other one behind the cactus. As he drew near, the man raced from behind the thick cactus and dashed farther from the roadway.

Taking these two from out here in the middle of nowhere and getting them to Lone Creek would be a chore. It took more work than the time Dango hauled the Braudan brothers in, after they tried to rob him, when he was hunting Gus the Pawnee.

After at least a couple hours and hard, sweat filled efforts, CW and Dango managed just that though.

CW finally filled Dango in that he knew who Ben West was, "He's the stagecoach driver. I already told you that Sam Harker was his shotgun rider."

"Well, who's the other stranger?"

"Can't say. Never saw him before. Don't know if he was a passenger on the stage. Not sure if he's the one who shot poor Sam, or if he was a victim himself in all this."

"What in cotton do you reckon is going on with them fellers? You think thy just got dehydrated? Or maybe delirious from going through whatever it was that cost Sam Harker to get a bullet in his forehead?"

"Can't really say without them being able to give us answers."

Then Dango asked the question that was more puzzling to them than all of that. Well, at least as puzzling. "What in the world happened to the stagecoach?"

"Good question. Weren't even any tracks out thar. Didn't appear that the stage was ever even thar."

Somehow, they knew it had been. Just couldn't figure out where it went, and why no tracks existed to prove it had even been at the sight of what they'd missed witnessing.

Chapter Fourteen

After breakfast, coffee, and time, the stage driver Ben West and the gambler were finally coming around.

Sheriff Lee and Dango questioned them until they'd asked the same questions several different ways and still didn't know much more than they had.

"I'm telling you Sheriff, it's all foggy to me. I remember me and Sam coming up the path, not far from that last stretch, to Lone Creek. After that, it's all muddled."

The gambler, who they figured out was named Jackson P. Strider, told an account that coincided with Ben's. "We were riding along at a good pace, then all of a sudden, y'all had us in here doing all this probing. All these interrogations. It's like I went to sleep, and the next thing I knew we were here in the sheriff's office."

A light seemed to go off in Dango's head, "Jackson P. Strider? As in the Jackson P. that's known from here to California?"

The gambler just nodded and looked proudly at the bounty hunter as they shook hands.

"You can call me Dango."

"Dango? As in the Dango Durango, the famous bounty hunter?"

"I don't know about all that."

Jackson P. Strider was known by Jackson P. He told everybody the P stands for poker.

Dango continued, "What's the legendary Jackson P. doing in this part of the country?"

"I do remember things before the trip here. I got a telegraph to play a high stakes game in Lone Creek. All the big names will be here."

Dango had followed gambling news, especially poker. He found this to be one of the ripe grounds for running across those he was looking for. He had met some mighty decent people at the tables and in the crowds. But, he had also determined some very dark scallywags liked to mingle among these fine upstanding poker gatherings.

"Oh yeah, which big names are expected?"

"Strychnine Jim, Big Bob Flowers, Hoot-Owl Chappy, and Lacy Laci."

"You don't say."

Dango's thoughts were running a hundred miles an hour at this news. How lucky could he be if Zeke Scott was really in the area, just as he'd heard. And how timely would it be if they crossed paths because of all the bustle stirred up by a big name poker game.

Dango knew enough about all of the players Jackson P. mentioned to know they all had stories behind their names.

Strychnine Jim had been accused of poisoning all the players around the table, one night, to make winning easier. It had been rumored that he gave them just enough to dull their senses.

Although never proven, it was not unlikely, given his reputation for playing dirty. Chitchat got around that it's a good thing he's as good with a gun as he is with the cards. He'd been called out more than once or twice to show his hand when suspected of cheating.

It was easy to see how Big Bob Flowers came by his name. He was big, his first name was Bob, and his last name was Flowers. His personality was as large as the rest of him.

Hoot-Owl Chappy had a heavy resemblance to a real life owl. His black, thick eyeglasses helped bring out that likeness.

Lacy Laci was named Laci and always wore lace. It was intriguing how a lady could wear so much lace and make it look so sensual. She had a way of using that to her advantage at the card table and away from the table.

Lacy Laci's blonde hair always looked like rollers had just been taken out. She loved wearing dresses, and had the appearance of a woman that would be seen sitting on a porch swing of a Victorian grand estate in Savannah, Georgia or Galveston, Texas. Her looks could be tremendously deceiving, as she was as ruthless as they came when at the gambling hall.

Even though Dango's mind was spinning, thinking of strategies for finding Zeke Scott, he didn't want to put all his cards on the table. "Sounds like a fun poker match. I'd like to be there for it."

"Heck yeah. Skills and money like nobody's seen in these parts."

Ben West and Sheriff Lee hadn't said much, but both of them had seemed very interested in the poker talk.

"Dango, I'll be bringing on some extra firepower if you wanna pin a badge on til after the poker game."

This same request had been made to Dango several times. He'd said yes to the offer more times than he cared to remember. Sometimes it had turned out in his favor. Other times, more harm had been done than good. It hadn't been too long ago that he'd been a short-term lawman, for a place called Timber Creek, over in Colorado.

"I think I'll sit this one out CW. I think y'all will do just okay with me staying the course for why I came here in the first place."

"I understand Dango. Just let me know if you change your mind."

Chapter Fifteen

"I'll tell you what; you give me the whole caboodle, and I'll see what I can do."

Slim One-Eye tried his best to look stern, but he knew the Hasinai Caddo warrior would pick up on his slight nervousness.

The warrior was in the same tribe Gus the Pawnee's group had belonged to, when they broke off and migrated to Oklahoma.

One-Eye rarely had any edginess, but he knew these Caddo definitely equaled in heartlessness to the Zulu Outlaws. His apprehension could lessen what he was trying to get in exchange from the Caddo.

The young Indian warrior finally responded after mulling the offer over, "I'll tell you what, you tell boss man if he wants to keep doing business with my tribe, then he better make it worth our while."

That was the longest sentence he'd had ever heard from this Indian. As broken as his use of the English language was, he knew him to be an intelligent wheeler dealer. He also knew the warrior spoke English a heck of a lot better than if One-Eye himself tried to communicate in the Caddo tongue.

The Caddo warrior wore a strand of feathers, at the end of a long braid of hair, that was ponytailed behind his head.

The sides of his head were completely bald to the skin.

His bronze face and chest were painted in colorful designs that One-Eye thought must mean something.

The Indian wore a shirt that looked like a pelt of buffalo hide that had been torn into strips. His stomach and chest were exposed, as the strips of the pelt mostly covered his back and sides. He had a sisal twine of bones around his neck and a ripped cloth tied around his forehead. Kicking the dirt, he turned as if to leave.

"Hold on War Cloud. You can have the whole thing. I'll meet you back here tomorrow ready to deal."

"You're mighty lucky I'd even consider coming back tomorrow. Many others'd love to get hands on these goods."

One-Eye realized the warrior known as War Cloud was telling the truth. Somehow, though, he managed to speak with more firmness than he felt. "Well, you ought to know there are many lining up for this too. You're not the only interested trader."

War Cloud quickly snapped, "Then go ahead! Trade somewhere else!"

"Whoa, whoa, whoa!" One-Eye countered, "Not so fast. I'm sure we can work this out. Just let me talk to Zeke. I'll be back tomorrow ready to make the switch with no more haggling."

"One more day Paleface. You better stick to your word when meet tomorrow, or I'll trade someone else."

That vibrated in the air. It sounded electric. Slim One-Eye would do all he could to convince Zeke of

the seriousness of how he handled this. He spurred his horse, intent to tell the boss these were Indians he did not want to mess with.

Chapter Sixteen

Those with a say in the matter had arguments among themselves about all the particulars that went into hosting a poker game of this magnitude in their town. They weren't even at a scale to warrant having the rail line come within less than a day away by coach from Lone Creek. However, for reasons unknown to them, this grand contest was slated to happen in their fine town.

One of the many details they had decided on was to begin the poker game in the evening. Some actually debated for it to start early in the morning. There had been heated talks covering the plusses and minuses. Eventually, the schedule was agreed upon, although not unanimously, to begin in the early evening.

The atmosphere was as jubilant as if the State Fair had come to Lone Creek. Men and women showed up, expecting to watch the masters of the cards. The only saloon in the town was the natural place to host such an event. Ladies didn't usually spend time here, and husbands that knew this to be their local watering hole were usually here against the wishes of their wives.

Some families even wanted to have children allowed inside during the poker match. The votes turned out against it, reasoning it was a bold enough move to allow all the wives to be admitted.

Black Jack stood at the end of a large, round table. He had one of the best smiles in the area and his big grin showed most of his teeth, as he shuffled the deck.

Black Jack had been born into slavery and named by the man who claimed ownership to his ma and pa. As soon as he was old enough to understand where his name came from, he sought to change it.

He didn't wait a day, after the war brought his freedom, to change it from Nathan Bedford to simply Black Jack.

When folks dared ask about his last name, he didn't even get into the details with them. Most people from that era didn't know who Nathan Bedford Forrest was. Most didn't realize he was a Confederate Army Lieutenant General in the Cavalry.

But Black Jack knew it. He had been raised in the home of a staunch Confederate supporter. He was easily the darkest person in town, so it wasn't difficult to come up with a new name. He just told folks, when they asked his name, that it was Black Jack. Hanging around the tables all the time helped that name stick.

His wide grin remained as he surveyed the players in front of him. Having his own idea of who would leave the table a big-time winner and who would lose big, he would devote his time to dealing without manipulating the outcome. Although, it would be strikingly effortless for him to do just that.

Black Jack had dealt cards to change tides in many games. His skills at dealing were to be marveled at.

He promised himself, however, this game would be determined by the abilities of the players and the choices they made.

Dango tried his best to mix in with the crowd that was gathered. He was told by Sheriff Lee that there'd never been this many folks in this establishment at one time. He stood and watched, hoping Zeke and his gang would see this as an opportunity to score big. He would be waiting when they showed up.

Strychnine Jim was dealt the first card of the match. Black Jack continued dealing around the table clockwise. The next card went to Lacy Laci, then Big Bob Flowers, Hoot-Owl Chappy, and finally Jackson P.

Black Jack kept dealing the cards until each player held two. He laid one card face up on the table in front of each player and the betting began. As Strychnine threw money into the pot, the other players kept watchful eyes on their drinks.

The largest personality at the table, Big Bob Flowers took a verbal jab to try and cause others to lose focus. "Say Jim, tell us the real story behind that rumor. I know you really couldn't have done that." He poked Lacy Laci gently with his forearm and everybody at the table laughed louder than Strychnine Jim cared for.

"My dear fellow, you can't believe everything you hear just because you hear it. I've never had to stoop to such sorts to win at what I do best. If I can't beat you with my sheer talents, then I just won't beat you."

Before Big Bob or the others could respond, Strychnine Jim continued. "But my talents are very real, make no mistake about that. Let's just see who comes out on top."

He added one more comment before allowing them to reply. "By the way, you all should make sure, and keep an eye on your drinks." He smiled almost as big as Black Jack when he said this.

Before three more up cards were laid on the table for each contestant by the dealer, the stakes were piling up. Each player seemed to almost salivate at the stack of greenbacks.

Black Jack threw the final card for each of them face down and betting continued. Each opponent wanted to send a message early by betting big and raking in a huge pot.

Jackson P. peeked at his cards once more and decided it would be best to wait til later for his big bluffs. Throwing his cards facedown, "I'll fold."

Lacy Laci had already folded, so three players were still in the running for the first hand. Strychnine Jim checked to Big Bob. "I'll kick in another five hundred."

He said this with an air of confidence. Strychnine Jim and Hoot-Owl Chappy had no idea if his confidence was genuine or not. They each had read many poker faces. However, Big Bob Flowers had spent many nights across Texas having his poker face read. He had perfected the look that was hard to break through and figure out.

Chappy was almost drooling, but he knew he'd already thrown in way too much on a bad hand. "Fold."

Strychnine Jim smiled as he realized it was just the two of them left in the hand. "I'll see your five hundred and raise another five hundred."

Expecting Big Bob to fold up at that move, he was taken by surprise as the big feller began counting money. "That's chicken feed Jim. How about we up the stakes?"

As he flung another thousand on the table, Strychnine Jim had a sickening feeling in his gut. He knew his pair of deuces couldn't take him any further in this opening hand. He tossed his cards down in disgust. "I fold."

Dango watched the entire first hand, noticing the cash mounding up on the table. He thought this would be a perfect time for Zeke and his gang to barge in and start a hold-up. He watched warily, half expecting them to do just that.

Big Bob Flowers laughed heartily. In one swoop motion, he raked in the heap of cash from the pot he'd just won and threw his cards face up on the table showing he would've been beat by Strychnine Jim's pair of twos.

The crowd gasped. Husbands explained to their wives what had just happened and how huge of a move that was. Players around the card table gritted their teeth and became resolute. Each of them had won big and lost big before. This was just the first hand.

There would be many more before it was over.

Big Bob nudged Lacy Laci again softly. "How ya like that little lady?"

This was just the kind of moves she wished for. Turning on the charm, they would be easy to distract while she collected her winnings.

And that's exactly what happened for several rounds of play. She had a way of making each of them think he was the only one she was making a play for. She would turn on the seducing and each of the men at the poker table couldn't help but flirt back with the pretty lady with all the lace. They had heard of her, knew her moves, and yet here they were being lured right into her trap. Playing her game.

After the first ten hands of play, the load of cash that had begun in front of Big Bob had moved to rest in front of Lacy Laci. Much more had been contributed to her earnings. "My my, I can barely see over all this money."

She giggled. The men weren't very amused anymore. "Just deal the cards Black Jack." Strychnine Jim callously demanded.

He smiled and did as ordered, thinking he could've been a little nicer instead of being so demanding. Nobody saw it, and Black Jack hadn't started the game intending to do this, but each time he dealt to Strychnine Jim, he slapped a card from the bottom of the deck. Thinking to himself, I'll teach him to not talk down to me like that.

Chapter Seventeen

Slim One-Eye felt like he gave a pretty convincing argument. He thought Zeke would realize how much of a mistake it would be to not make the deal with War Cloud. Riding together, they would be at the meeting point soon.

"You reckon he'll really show up alone?"

"Last time we met, as far as I could tell, it was just him and me."

Zeke was agitated as he responded, "I don't care about last time! You didn't get the deal done last time. I'm only concerned about what happens today. Do you think he'll come by himself? Or will he have other Injuns with 'im?"

"How in Sam Hill am I supposed to answer that Zeke? Do I look like a mind reader?"

Zeke wasn't used to others being so insolent with him. One-Eye had been a thorn in his flesh ever since he had met him. If he didn't see him as an outlaw who brought a lot to the table, he'd kill him right here and roll him down a cliff somewhere.

"You ain't gotta be no danged mind reader One-Eye, to tell me how you think it's gonna turn out. Which one is it? Do you think this War Cloud will be by himself or not?"

"Yes Zeke! Yes I do! I think he'll come all by himself!

There won't be another Indian around for a thousand miles!"

Zeke barked, "Now, you're just messing with me! Just forget it! If he comes alone, so be it. If he brings every Caddo with him that's living, that'll be ok too."

"There he is boss."

The two men looked ahead and saw the one called War Cloud sitting atop his majestically ornamented stallion. The horse had enough feathers draping his sides to decorate at least a couple dozen warriors. War Cloud had similar feathers adorning his own braided pony-tail.

"I thought you were coming alone pale face."

"War Cloud, this is my boss Zeke Zulu Scott."

The Caddo Indian let out a piercing shrill that startled Zeke and One-Eye. They both jumped in their saddles and instinctively reached for their firearms.

Their reflexes caused them to bring their pistols up to aim directly at the Indian. As quick as their impulses were, before they had them raised, he already had his rifle pointed in the direction of both of them.

"Calm down. Put firearms down. I was just giving honorary warrior cry for being in presence of great Zeke Zulu Scott."

Zeke and One-Eye each formed small smiles as they lowered their weapons. As War Cloud dropped his rifle beside his waist, Zeke lifted his own head and screamed towards the sky, trying his best to sound like the Caddo warrior had sounded.

War Cloud wasn't a bit alarmed, yet a smile bent slightly upward on his face.

"Are you men here to make deal? Or will you waste more of time?"

"Did you come alone?"

War Cloud stared intently at Zeke after the question. "Why do you ask such thing? What do you have up sleeve Dark Outlaw?"

Zeke took a liking to the moniker the Indian warrior had just labeled him with. He growled, "Dark Outlaw? I like it."

"Do you like enough to answer question Dark Outlaw?"

"I just wanna make sure you don't have a herd of help waiting to ambush us after the trade."

"And you think I would tell you if I did? For one thing, we are not a herd, we are a tribe! What nonsense coming from one of such reputation."

Zeke aimed his revolver with lightning speed at War Cloud, his finger on the trigger, glaring at the Indian with an intent to kill.

"Who do you think you're talking to you red-belly galoot? I don't know who you're used to running your gums at that way, but it shore ain't me!"

"Boss, slow down! Let's think this out."

One-Eye consoled Zeke for a few minutes, just like he'd done several times in the past. Usually, it didn't work. Usually, somebody ended up dead even

after all the words he used to try and smooth out

Zeke's feathers, that had been ruffled.

He tried every angle he could think of in just a few frantic moments. Whispering, "Boss, don't let this Injun get you all riled up. You shoot him, we'll have every Caddo Indian around coming gunning for us."

Zeke defiantly and loudly spit back, "You think I'm scared of a Caddo? I ain't afraid of all the Caddos in the whole wide world!"

Finally, somehow, something One-Eye said clicked. Zeke lowered his weapon, carefully watching War Cloud, making sure he didn't react by raising his.

"I'll tell you what War Cloud, let's not haggle around here. You take the entire kaboot, and give us what we came after."

"What's this word you use? Kaboot?" I don't savvy that word."

"Okay, let me simplify it for you. You take the entire stagecoach, the whole thing.

It's still in one piece, even has the wheels on it. In exchange, we get the rifles and drugs. The peyote, coca leaves, poppy plants, opiates, morphine, and mushrooms. All of it."

War Cloud didn't hesitate. It was as though he knew exactly what terms he would agree to already. "Done. You leave coach. Men from tribe will get and take."

"So you do have help nearby?"

"Do you think I'm crazy man Dark Outlaw?"

"Let's just get the stuff in our wagon so we can get the heck out of here."

Zeke and One-Eye loaded the military grade rifles and drugs as quickly as possible and headed out. Next stop Claster's Cavern.

Chapter Eighteen

Back at the caverns, Zeke and Slim One-Eye met back up with the rest of the crew. At the moment Zeke was having an overdue talk with Clankie Claster. Most of the discourse had been about the recent dealings with War Cloud. Some of the gang thought it had gone down just as they would have planned it. Others would've rather done some things differently.

"I just don't think the whole thing should've been parted with still in one piece. If the wrong people see it, they can trace it back to us. That's the only thing I would've changed about the deal."

Zeke was still having a very hard time getting used to some of his men saying what they thought, just because they thought it.

"Clankie, ain't nobody gonna put two and two together and match that stagecoach with us. And besides that, what if they do? What're they gonna do about it? Absolutely nothing. Not a dadblamed thing!"

Zeke threw the hammer he was holding. It struck a wall of the cave and bounced off, clanging sounds ricocheting through the cavern.

He continued, "And besides that, who in the world made you overseer of the Zulu Outlaws? I'm getting sick and tired of you trying to outdo me!"

"Outdo you? What does that mean Zeke?" He took a breath and continued, "What does that even mean?"

"You know good and well what I mean Clankie! Here lately, everywhere we go, every danged job we do, you've been doing your best to kill more folks than me, to stir up more ruckus than me! Don't think I don't know what's going on. You're a decent outlaw and all, but you don't have near what it takes to run an outfit the likes of this!"

"I don't know what you mean Zeke! It's not my fault I've been causing more damage lately than you. Sounds like you just need to up your game."

Clankie full out expected Zeke to pick the hammer up and throw it again. Maybe even at him. He braced for it, but instead Zeke stuck to talking instead, in his deep, growly voice.

"Just listen to reason; I've been doing a lot of thinking lately."

Before he continued, Clankie cut in, You've been known to do a lot of that as long as I've known you."

"Yeah, but this is big. You know as leader of the Zulu Outlaws, I reckon I should be the one getting all the big scores, all the glory kills. It really ought to be me that serves out most of the violence. I even have a term for it."

Clankie almost chuckled. "Oh yeah Zeke, what's that?"

"I've been thinking, since we're the Zulu Outlaws, we need what I call an Outlaw Code."

"Outlaw Code? What in tarnation is that Zeke? Sounds good whatever it is."

"Outlaw Code. We'll come up with codes that outlaws should go by and write them down. Such as, if one gang is in a bank holding it up, and another gang comes in to rob it, they gotta leave and let the gang that was already there finish the job."

Clankie laughed a huge belly laugh. "That's one of the funniest things you've ever said Zeke." He was still laughing the whole time he was talking. "But it's brilliant too. I like it. As a matter of fact, I like it a lot."

"That's smart of you Clankie. And I think the first thing on top of the list of the Outlaw Code is that gang members can't inflict more damage and more violence than the gang leader."

Clankie smiled at that. "I'm all for that Zeke, but all I can say about it is you better up your game, because I'm bent on upping mine."

Thus, in Claster's Cave on the outskirts of Lone Creek, Texas during a heated discussion between two desperadoes, the Outlaw Code was born.

Chapter Nineteen

Zeke and Clankie had filled in the rest of the gang on the new Outlaw Code they'd formed. They were all in with the notion, and this morning when they woke up, it seemed like a good time to put it to the test.

It was one of the prettiest mornings this part of Texas had seen in a while. The temperature was seventy degrees. It felt exactly like sixty-five with a mild breeze blowing from the south.

It was still early, but the temperature wouldn't climb over seventy-two today. As the riders left Claster's Cavern, they each breathed the impeccable air of knowing they were about to be part of something big. It felt like they'd ridden out hundreds of times to spill their fierce hatred on those deserving. Yet, this time was different. Purpose was higher. Even in the heart of outlaws, a sense of resolve and reason sprung from their dark souls. The code provided that sense of fulfilling a higher calling.

If these highly gifted men would run this notion by Dango Durango or Sheriff CW Lee, those two lawmen would see the foolishness in it. But the Zulu Outlaws, each of them, had a new drive, one that invigorated their passion to kill. That drive was the Outlaw Code.

Each of them knew where they were heading. The employees and customers at Ernie's Trading Square would be touched by a happening that would change them forever. That is, the ones who lived through it.

Ernie Session had swept off the front stoop of his business, every morning, since he established the place. This morning was no different. Erlene, his wife, was inside greeting the crowd of regulars already milling about.

Erlene knows what it's like to be a customer at Ernie's Trading Square, and she knows the importance of making each one feel special. She used to be a regular customer herself when the first Mrs. Session was still living.

It wasn't long after Ernie's first wife died, that he got hitched with Erlene and she moved into the house and took her place helping him run the business.

Erlene was at least twenty years younger than Ernie. Folks talked, but that didn't deter them. Ernie and Erlene reckoned if the two of them were okay with it, nobody else had a say in it.

Ernie's first wife had always been harsh with the regulars. He had loved her dearly for all her wonderful ways. But he recognized Erlene's compassionate qualities the place had always needed.

It was that compassion that brought her out to the porch this morning. "Hun, Mr. Eckols needs fifty pounds of potatoes, but I can't seem to locate any."

Ernie quit sweeping immediately to head in and show Erlene where the sacks of potatoes were and to get someone to fetch them for Mr. Eckols.

Before he made it to the door, Erlene's eyes showed him something wasn't right. Looking behind him, he saw what caused her eyes to twinkle in fear. He didn't know who they were yet, but seven men, of different skin colors, riding in with guns drawn and handkerchiefs covering their faces couldn't spell anything but trouble.

Ernie didn't wait for the shooting to start. He knew as sure as his love burned for Erlene, that trouble was in the making. He charged to the counter just inside the front door, yelling the whole time for Erlene to get down!

Grabbing his Winchester, he raced back outside. The outlaws hadn't begun shooting yet. Ernie fired the first round. He blasted four times, bam, bam, bam, bam! He wasn't sure which one of them found its mark. Out of four shots, one of the outlaws fell.

One of the Lujak twins got a fatal gut shot and fell from his horse. Zeke never called them by their first name, but Beau Lujak would later tell Zeke it was Sage Lujak, who died that day. The twins had been inseparable until a bullet from a storekeeper's rifle severed their togetherness.

Ernie ran back inside and ducked for cover. Finding a window nearby, be continued firing, hoping to take out each and every one of them. Gunshots began coming from the outlaws. The sound of bullets drumming the store exterior was deafening. Glass shattered and sprayed inside and outside of the store.

Ernie stayed behind cover and kept shooting. He hadn't hit another human target besides Sage Lujak, but he fired nonstop. He wasn't really aiming, didn't want to chance looking up from his hiding spot.

Ernie didn't know it, but while he was blindly firing from his concealment, Zeke, Slim One-Eye, Desert Joe, Copperhead Cooper, and Clankie Claster had circled around and stormed in the rear of the place. Before he was aware of what was happening, they stood behind him, guns drawn, pointed right at him.

Erlene screamed, "Ernie, lookout!"

He turned and immediately knew he had no recourse but to give up and turn over his rifle. All the clientele in the establishment were ducking for cover as well. They didn't dare come out until Zeke fired in the air and demanded everybody to reveal themselves.

They came from various hiding spots. Including Ernie and Erlene, there were twenty-four of them. Copperhead Cooper was busy with his duster bag for a while. He had customers putting everything, except the clothes they had on, in the bag.

Zeke was tempted to kill everybody in the place to make up for the Lujak twin being murdered by the shopkeeper. Instead, he had another idea, "Herd 'em all in the owner's office. Every last one of 'em. Cram 'em in tight."

The outlaw gang had all twenty-four of them packed in Ernie's little office. Zeke went to work with something he had recently begun doing on holdups.

While he was doing that, Desert Joe was working on a handwritten sign that read The Zulu Outlaws Were Here. This was as original in the 1800s as the Outlaw Code.

Zeke felt extremely proud of himself that day. He would get acclaim for all twenty-four victims. He wouldn't waste bullets to kill them, but he would leave them to be found, out of their minds, by the authorities. Hopefully, he could give them enough of what he got from War Cloud to make that bewildered state permanent.

After he had them all secured with the sisal rope, he forced them at gunpoint to ingest several different drugs. He had coca leaves, poppy plants, opiates, morphine, mushrooms, and peyote at his disposal.

For this stick-up, he decided to go with the peyote dissolved in berry wine mixed with mushrooms. Peyote contains mescaline which is known to cause hallucinations. This combined with the psychedelic properties of the mushrooms and the alcohol would be dangerously potent.

These arrogant business owners and their customers. Zeke saw them as big-headed and superior minded just because they succeeded at something positive in life. To him, they were prey and he was the predator at the top of the food chain. If he has his way, they will have extreme illusions and be sick out of their minds.

The drugs working through their systems would cause them to experience a feeling of nothingness.

They would see and hear things that weren't there. Feeling and truly believing they were almost dead would be a real sensation, because it was a very real possibility that this mixture could cause death to occur suddenly.

Their hearts would go from a range of tachycardia where they would beat very rapidly, to a dangerously slow rhythm that would nearly send them into a coma.

Zeke's deranged thoughts put an involuntary grin on his hardened face at these thoughts. Those who rode with him had the same grin for the same irrational reasons.

Zeke was certain to ride high for a long time after this. Clankie Claster would be left in his dust. The Outlaw Code was alive and well.

It took a while to get all twenty-four of 'em crowded into the tiny office and filled with the narcotics. Once accomplished, Zeke slammed the door shut, and the Zulu Outlaws filled their wagon with everything they could take from the establishment and headed out.

Dango and Sheriff Lee had both been out of earshot that morning. Zeke and his men would be back at the cave before the room packed with doped up people would be discovered.

Chapter Twenty

The poker game had gone late into the night. Lacy Laci's seductress ways had accomplished exactly what she intended. How could these skilled poker professionals fall to her tricks and act like young boys with no worldly understanding? She didn't care to explain it. She only knew it worked and would use this to her advantage every time.

She had stretched them all very thin and would've thrown the knockout punch, but shortly after two-thirty in the morning, the agreement of the group was to go to their rooms and rest for a while before reconvening after daylight to finish out the match.

It was around eight-fifteen when the players began showing up at the same table they had played on the night before. Black Jack was stationed at one end of the round table, just as though he'd been there all night.

Dango was back, situated near the table, but far enough away to not draw attention to himself if Zeke and his men stormed in to rob the poker players of their winnings. Conversation started up right away. Big Bob Flowers seemed to always get the jump on the rest of the players at the table no matter where he was. The same thing happened this morning, "What'd y'all have for breakfast this morning?"

Lacy Laci answered first. "I found this fantastic place on Main Street. The owners, Harold and Lois

Stone said they personally fixed my meal for me."

Hoot-Owl Chappy mentioned he'd seen her in there when he was having his breakfast. She playfully teased, starting already, "You were in there when I was? Why you should've come on over to my table and ate with me."

Hoot-Owl almost blushed and said he hadn't wanted to bother her that early.

Before she could let him know he wouldn't have been a bother, Jackson P. cut in, "I had my customary breakfast of whisky straight this morning."

They all laughed as Black Jack began to deal the cards. Lacy Laci's greenbacks were heaped in front of her. All four men had short stacks in front of them.

Before the first round of betting began, one of the citizens of Lone Creek rushed in the door. "Has anybody seen the sheriff? There's a ton of folks over at Ernie's place, gone mad!"

Dango walked with a purpose over to the man. "Sheriff Lee should be here any time now. He hasn't made it yet."

"Well somebody's gotta come and see what's going on! Ernie Session killed an outlaw! The whole place was robbed! Everybody that's left there is out of their mind!"

This all sounded way too familiar to Dango. "Let's go." Before they walked out, he instructed those near the poker table, "Somebody let the sheriff know what's going on when he gets here."

Chapter Twenty-One

When Dango arrived at Ernie's Trading Square, he found the place just as the man had described it. Sage Lujak's body still lay in the dusty roadway out front of the place. Ernie, Erlene, their staff, and all the customers were still packed in the tiny office.

Emotions in that small office were varied. Some of them were laughing hysterically. Others were crying relentlessly. Some were hiding in corners. Others were up front trying everything they could do to get the attention of anybody who would listen.

It was, without a doubt, one of the worst scenes Dango had ever witnessed. And he had been a lot of places, seen a lot. He didn't know where to begin helping this group. Before he mapped out a plan in his mind, Sheriff Lee walked briskly into the store.

"Dango, any idea what's gone on here?"

"Not at all sheriff. I know there's a man dead in the street. There're over twenty in here acting like they've completely lost it. Kind of like when we found that stagecoach driver and gambler on the stage route."

"You don't say."

"This seems worse though. As bad as I thought ol' Ben and Jackson were when we first found them; this seems a ton worse."

"I'll tell you the truth Dango, I don't rightly know where to start."

"How about we fetch the doc? Maybe he'll have a clue what to do with all these delirious men and women."

"Maybe so. Let's try it. I'm sure glad there were no kids here this morning."

"Well, whoever did this, whatever they did to these individuals, I don't think they would've minded if there would have been children involved."

"Probably not. I'll send Luke after the doc while we try and calm these poor souls."

It was a wonder Dango and Sheriff Lee could have a civilized conversation while all this was happening. It was heart wrenching. The two lawmen tried their best to stay composed, but it was challenging them like nothing they'd experienced.

Both of them walked into the room full of people who seemed to be wild, brain damaged, uncontrollable, mentally unstable.

"Dango, I know most of these folks. All of them are decent, upstanding people."

"I don't doubt it CW. I just hope they will become those kinds of people again. Right now, it looks impossible."

Chapter Twenty-Two

Doc Gillon arrived, expecting the worse. Luke had spared no details. However, Doc was not prepared for what he saw when they got to Ernie's place.

Sheriff Lee and Dango were in the room with the bewildered people. They seemed out of place with the others. It was easy to recognize they didn't have a clue how to help the victims.

They talked for a few minutes, wondering how they could help. Without knowing exactly what was causing the insanity, they didn't actually have a good plan yet.

Then another surprise happened. A young, brown haired little boy about ten years old came out of nowhere. He had been hiding the entire time, ever since the Zulu Outlaws entered the place this morning.

"Little Ben, where in the world did you come from?"

The boy seemed too shocked to answer the sheriff. As hard as it was for Doc, citizen Luke, Dango, and Sheriff Lee to cope with what was happening, the child was dazed much more.

After about another hour of scratching their heads, a plan was formed. Doc had suggested that Ernie's Trading Square be turned into a makeshift hospital.

Doc would stay all day and night if needed, to tend as best he could. Sheriff Lee would go round up a posse of men to come stand guard at the place. Then, Dango

and the sheriff would take the young boy to the jail and try and get him soothed enough to provide some information. Anything would be better than what they already knew.

Several hours passed before little Ben spoke a word of anything that had happened at Ernie's place. Finally, after much gentle effort by the lawmen, he filled them in that several very bad men, who looked like outlaws, made all the people take some kind of stuff they called drugs. They mixed something with alcohol and made them drink it. Then they all started acting very weird. It scared him very bad.

He was glad when the sheriff and Dango showed up. He was feeling some better, but he wished his ma and pa would be better soon.

Chapter Twenty-Three

As Dango rode hard toward Claster's Cavern, he had more than enough for one man to think about on his mind. He was weighted down and could tell the load was bearing down on him.

His thoughts included all those fine folks at Ernie's Trading Square who had fallen prey to Zeke Scott and his heinous gang. That was the next thing taking up space in his brain, the Zulu Outlaws.

Riding along at a fast pace, the mental strain bore down on him. His mind was cluttered with imaginations of permanent brain damage to all those people. He wondered if those monstrous outlaws would ever be stopped. How many more innocent people would lose their lives?

The burden of the thoughts, eventually came out as a silent conversation with someone greater than himself. He prayed to God, who he knew had to be listening, and talked about all his thoughts.

He told the Great Creator of the Universe that he's come to a place where it's easier to believe in Hell than Heaven. After all the bad he's witnessed, Hell makes a lot of sense. He didn't struggle at all thinking the likes of Zeke Scott and his outlaws would go to a place of torment for eternity.

His thoughts continued flowing in the form of a prayer. He hoped, wished, prayed that Ernie and Erlene

and all those employees and customers of Ernie's place would get okay, even if it took a miracle. He knew he couldn't make it happen himself, but surely God could do it.

His prayer ended with a request for all those in that outlaw gang to be arrested or even killed. Somehow, someway, Dango petitioned the good Lord, use me to stop those dark souls.

Dango did not have it in him to see a clear path for these prayers to be answered. He didn't really have the foresight or visual anticipation for the ones who had been drugged so seriously to ever recover. He couldn't fathom how he could ride into those caverns and bring out all those hard-case outlaws alone.

He was keen enough to realize that he couldn't see this all working out like he wanted. So, he decided to not put his hope in only his visual awareness. He had to let his faith stretch and trust in God. Okay Lord, if it's going to work out, it's going to have to be You. I know it and You know it.

He began to realize a sense of peace. With all that had gone wrong and all that still could go bad, a peace washed over him and drove him to forge forward, realizing he indeed was not alone. He would have to put a whole lot of action with the faith he was trying to use.

He would give it all he had though, fight as hard as it took. Somehow, he knew he wasn't alone.

Chapter Twenty-Four

Desert Joe had told Zeke Scott that Beau Lujak was distraught over the death of his brother and said he was going to leave. The last thing he had said to him when they left Ernie's Trading Square was something about heading back to Canada. He had disappeared. Surely, he was good to his word and was miles away, somewhere between Lone Creek, Texas and Canada by now.

The frenzy at Claster's Cavern seemed like a bee hive. The activity in the cave entrance was stirred to its fullest. Desert Joe, Slim One-Eye, and Copperhead Cooper were getting the latest coach they had taken from the stage line, out near the Louisiana state line, ready for dealing.

They would strip the buggy, and trade it for parts near Oklahoma. From there, the parts would be moved further into Kansas and sold to the men who were in charge of keeping the line going, through that state, westward to the Pacific Ocean.

Zeke and Clankie were packaging the drugs the gang had gotten from the Caddo. They would keep some to use during their hold-ups. The rest they'd sell for a massive profit. These would be marketed east, from Louisiana all the way to the Atlantic Ocean and up the eastern seaboard.

Meanwhile, Dango and Twilight rode along heading on a course due northwest towards the caverns.

Little Ben had been a great help in providing information to give Dango a starting point. He wasn't sure if he'd really find the outlaws there, but he had to begin somewhere.

Riding along at a steady pace, he wasn't quite sure what he'd find at the caves. For that matter, he wasn't even certain what his line of attack would be once he got there if he did come upon the savages he was searching for.

Dango and Twilight were riding along, ascending up a moderate slope. Trees had become sparse this far from Lone Creek. You'd see a solitary tumbleweed or Joshua tree here and there. If you were looking to find a cactus, you could spot a barrel Saguaro without looking very hard. Sagebrush grew from a foot tall to nearly six feet in this area. It was not flowering and did not appear that it had any time recently.

They rose over a gentle slope and leveled out on what looked like a considerable plain that went on forever. Up ahead, far on the horizon, Dango could tell the plain began to rise even higher. He sensed the caverns would have an entrance somewhere on that ascent.

Unexpectedly, at the same time he took in the acreage he was traveling on, he was flabbergasted at the enormous circle of Caddo warriors that seemed to suddenly have him surrounded. The circle of Injuns must have been at least a mile in circumference.

Each of the many Indians wore a strand of feathers braided and ponytailed behind their head. The sides of their heads were completely bare to the skin.

Each had a bronze complexion and colorful patterns were painted on each chest and face. Their horses were adorned with bands of feathers flowing on each side.

Dango would soon discover these were Caddo warriors. Each of them wore shreds of buffalo hides that had been torn into strips. Their bellies and chests were visible underneath the buffalo hide garments.

One of the Indians broke from the circle and rode hard to approach Dango. The bounty hunter tried to take a non-aggressive posture and wondered how, in the name of cotton, this fit into the prayer he had recently made. Suddenly, his sense of calm and peace seemed to be ripped from him.

The approaching Indian reined his horse to an abrupt stop in front of the white stranger. Dust blew into the air. In halting English, he spoke, "Paleface, why you travel in these lands?"

Dango wasn't sure if he should spill the truth to him or make something up. He'd never been good at making things up quickly. It probably would have been a good trait to have in his line of work, but he'd never practiced it enough to have it as a tool in his arsenal.

"I hear tell there's an outlaw gang holed up somewhere in the caverns northwest of here. Gotta head honcho they call Zeke Scott."

"Outlaw gang? Why you have concern with them?"

"They're wanted for many crimes in the area, from stealing to murder."

"This outlaw gang you speak of, what do if find them?"

"Haven't quite figured that part out yet. Hopefully take 'em in for trial. They'll probably all hang." Dango kept one eye on the circle of Indians in the near distance.

"Wait here. Be right back."

The stern tone of the Caddo's voice ensured Dango he meant what he said. The plethora of Indians encircled around them added validity to that claim.

War Cloud raced back to the circle of his people and spoke with some of them for just a few minutes. It seemed like forever to the white man waiting for him to return.

Dango had a considerable hankering to learn what the next minutes would bring. As he was mulling it over, the Indian broke from his conversation and headed back.

The Indian got right to the point, raising his hand as a sign of solidarity, "My name is War Cloud. You pass this way once.

If survive what you are heading into, we allow passage back through these lands. After that, don't get caught these lands again."

Dango had a sense the Indian named War Cloud meant every word of it. "Thanks friend. My name is Dango Durango.

If I make it back this way and get out of this area alive,

I don't reckon I intend to travel this path again."

"I will pray to the Great Spirit that you have a safe journey."

Dango wasn't right sure if he and War Cloud prayed to the same God or not. But he did mightily appreciate the Indian's offer of prayer instead of the many other ways this could have turned out today.

Chapter Twenty-Five

As Dango rode up the ascent, keeping a watchful eye for a cave entrance, his thoughts were filled with doubts and wondering. How in cotton would he bring this whole gang in by himself? Just him and Twilight?

He'd been on the outnumbered side many a time and somehow had always come out on top. It hadn't always been easy, and some of the times he'd swear he'd had help from above. He was hoping this would be one of those times. A nagging doubt wouldn't go away though.

Riding along, a faint noise began hitting his ears. A distant, banging sound. Instinctively, he followed the clatter, wondering what would be making such a clamor way out here.

With Sage Lujak dead and Beau Lujak heading hard for Canada, the outlaw gang hadn't even given thought to replacing their roles outside with other lookouts. Dango was riding up to Claster Caverns entrance with the Zulu Outlaws inside being none the less wary.

They didn't have a clue he was just outside. He had a suspicion that he was getting closer to the nasty gang, but couldn't be a hundred percent positive of it. He was sure he'd find out real soon though and was building up for the one to five odds.

The outlaws knew the lay of the place inside the caves.

He'd try to coax them outside if he could. Another, thought, even though it was daylight outside, he was sure it would get mighty dark inside those caverns. He did not want to get killed in those caverns and that be his final resting place.

Getting closer to the banging racket. Clang! Clang! Over and over, it reverberated. Drawing nearer, it sounded like iron hitting iron. Clang! Clang! Someone was doing some mighty heavy hitting.

Dango reckoned he'd just sneak in and hopefully take them out one by one. Or, if it came to it, have an all-out glory blazing shootout and kill 'em all without getting so much as a scrape himself.

Inching his way into the cave, he found it wasn't as dark in the front entrance as he'd expected. The gang had makeshift lights burning through the front room of the caverns. He slid in and found cover behind a stalagmite that must've been in the cave entry for years.

He peeked around the salty dome and saw the man banging his hammer on the wheel of a stage coach. Planning to crouch and silently get to him before being noticed, he began edging that way.

Dango didn't get ten feet from the rock pillar he'd been hiding behind before the outlaw noticed him and stopped hammering.

The sound of the hammering when it stopped was attention getting. He'd been at it for so long.

The next sound was just as conspicuous. Zeke fired in the

direction of the stranger in his hideout. The shot took a chunk out of the cave wall behind Dango.

Not seeing any practical option, Dango fired back while working his way backward, hoping to find cover behind the same salty, domed spike he'd been behind. Before he could get there though, the other Zulu Outlaws showed up from farther in the caverns.

All of a sudden, he was inside the caves with Zeke Scott, Clankie Claster, Slim One-Eye, Desert Joe, and Copperhead Cooper. They were moving to form a flank around him. The only move in his favor was backwards toward the cave entry. Although, now it wouldn't be an entry, it would be his exit.

With six guns firing, his and five others, bullets were ricocheting everywhere. He ducked and backed out as fast as he could without stumbling, not even thinking of how this was going to end in the capture of the bandits.

Finally, after what seemed to be forever, he backed out of the cave completely. The outlaws kept following. Looking up in the sunlight, he couldn't believe his eyes. How in cotton could he be surrounded? Zulu Outlaws coming from the cave after him, and now behind him, just outside the cave, were at least fifty Indian warriors!

Chapter Twenty-Six

Dango couldn't believe it! It was hard enough to swallow retreating from a cave with the outlaws he was hunting chasing him. But now, it was the epitome of being between a rock and a hard place. How had he let himself get into such a position? He hadn't seen this coming at all.

With outlaws flanking him from the front and Indians circling him from the rear, he scampered, until finally he didn't know if it would be best to go toward the outlaws and fight or go toward the Indians and fight. Then, as he figured it'd be better to go after five outlaws instead of fifty Indians, out of nowhere a bullet cracked past his head and knocked Desert Joe off of his horse!

Another bullet whizzed by and plummeted into the ground just in front of Slim One-Eye. It didn't take much for Dango to realize the Indians weren't fighting him. They were after the desperadoes!

He turned his attention back to giving hostilities to the ones he had come after. Shooting round after round until his revolver was empty, he reloaded as he started firing with his repeating rifle.

The gunfight seemed to go on forever. At times during the heat of the skirmish, time seemed to slow down as things went in slow motion.

Other moments seemed to speed up and things flew in fast forward. Bullets hummed, and hissed. Flesh was punctured and blood spurted.

After an infinity of deafening booms and yelling, slow motion and fast forward seemed to collide. Indians were shrilling in the Caddo dialect. The various cultures of the Zulu Outlaws were distinctly heard through earsplitting profanities being bellowed in the air.

Dango and Twilight maintained their skilled bearing, going through the motion of doing what they'd done many times.

As the fighting began to slow, there were several wounded. Eight Caddo Indians were on the ground injured. Desert Joe was the only fatality. All of the rest of the Zulu Outlaws were hurt and bleeding. They were bad off enough that the fight was out of them for now. Each of them laid on the ground outside Claster's Cave squirming in pain, cursing, wishing they could get to more ammunition. None of them were in shape to go get more bullets, wouldn't have the wherewithal to do any more fighting today, even if they could fetch more ammo.

Dango and Twilight were in the middle of the circle of the conflict, and somehow neither of them was so much as scratched. Dango blamed it on answered prayer. He'd find out more in just a few minutes.

A familiar red face galloped up to him, "Friend, you okay?"

Dango noticed War Cloud right away. "I'm fine. Looks like some of your men are injured."

"My people have great medicine. They will be well."

With outlaws that needed tending to and hurt Indians, Dango just had to know one more thing. "Why'd you come here? Why'd you and your tribe help me?"

"You hero to us. You man who went after Gus the Pawnee. He killed my father's second wife. Gus was my step-brother. He killed my step-mother. Only mother I ever knew. My real mother died when I was very young."

Dango remembered that Gus the Pawnee had indeed killed his own white mother, who had married a Caddo Indian. "Thanks friend. I owe you a great deal."

"You repay by taking outlaws from this cave."

Dango replied, "I'll hitch them to their own horses and tie them off in a caravan. Then I'll lead the whole mess of them into Lone Creek to stand trial."

"Sounds good. If you hang them on the way, that is good too."

Chapter Twenty-Seven

It took somewhat longer to travel the road back to Lone Creek than it had taken to get to the caverns. Dango had ridden alone from Lone Creek to Claster's Cave. Now, he had four bloody outlaws tied up and riding in a line.

They rode along, five horses, each with a person on top of him. Dango rode on Twilight. Zeke, One-Eye, Clankie, and Copperhead were each strapped over his own steed. Ghengis didn't seem too proud today as Zeke Zulu Scott was laid over him, tied securely.

Dango had found enough drugs, weapons, and stagecoach parts back at Claster's Cavern to prove how big the Zulu Outlaws illegal empire was. There was a cache of rifles that only military men should have possession of. Stagecoach parts appeared to have been taken from several different stage lines.

Drugs that he discovered included the peyote with mescaline from the Chihuahuan Desert. There were also coca leaves and poppy plants. These could be chewed or dissolved in alcohol such as berry wine for effect.

Also, there were opiates, morphine, and hallucinogenic mushrooms. Dango was beginning to put two and two together, to realize what was going on with all those decent folks back at Ernie's Trading Square. He realized his prayer for the arrest of the

Zulu Outlaws had been answered in a magnificent way.

He could only hold on to hope that those back at Ernie's place have just as great of an outcome. He couldn't help the concern and worry he had. He'd seen a lot of bad guys killed or brought to justice. However, he'd rarely witnessed somebody in as bad a shape as all of them being cured. His heavy thoughts were stabbing at him, it'd be near like somebody coming back from the dead for them all to get better. His thoughts continued rambling through his mind, and I ain't never seen that happen.

Chapter Twenty-Eight

"There's a parade! There's a parade!"

Little Ben had taken a liking to Sheriff Lee. Ever since he'd spent time with the sheriff and Dango, he'd thought of them as someone who really cares. He hoped they'd help his ma and pa.

The sheriff, who'd been tacking another wanted poster on the outside of the hoosegow came around the corner to see what all the noise was.

"What's got you making all this uproar Son?"

"There's a parade!"

The sheriff looked up the road and saw the convoy of six horses. He recognized as they drew near that Dango was leading the way. The men who were hogtied to the horses were cursing and wriggling, trying their best to free themselves.

Twilight came to a stop just before reaching the boardwalk in front of the jail. Dango hopped from the saddle, "Afternoon CW."

"Afternoon Dango." Sheriff Lee said with a grin. "I see you've had a successful trip. Where'd you catch up with them at?"

"Yeah, you might say that CW. I found 'em right where Little Ben said I would."

He hadn't said that loud enough for the outlaws to know what he was saying.

Zeke hollered, "You talking about us Lawman? You untie these knots and let's see how tough you are!"

Sheriff Lee told Little Ben, "Run on home Son. We've got jail work to take care of."

The ten-year old didn't argue one bit. As much as he'd like to stay and help the sheriff and Dango take care of the jail business, he had a ton too much respect to back talk. He ran on after hollering, "See y'all later."

Dango had carried extra shackles with him on the bounty hunt. Sheriff Lee began loosening ropes on the bad men and pulling them from the horses. Each of them was bound in the irons Dango had put on them, and the sheriff prodded them towards the jail.

Getting the hard cases inside, he led them each to a separate cell. It hadn't been this noisy and chaotic in a while at the calaboose.

Zeke, still the dangerous killer he'd been before his arrest, spouted off, "You better burn that rope or hide it real good. If I get my hands on it, I'm gonna tie you up with it and beat your brains out!"

Sheriff CW Lee didn't hesitate as he immediately replied, "I ain't gonna burn it or hide it. I plan to use it to hang y'all with soon as the trial's over."

Zeke Scott, Slim One-Eye, Clankie Claster, and Copperhead Cooper continued getting loud, swearing at everything in sight. They mocked the sheriff's words, but little did they know, he meant every word of it.

Chapter Twenty-Nine

A week later, the poker players had reconvened to finish what they'd started. They took a vote and decided Lone Creek was too much for them. So, here they were, on a paddlewheel boat, steaming down the Mississippi.

The Creole Princess had seen her share of visitors come aboard. Lacy Laci, Strychnine Jim, Big Bob Flowers, Hoot-Owl Chappy, and Jackson P. fit right up near the top of the list. The president himself had ridden this massive paddleboat just for leisure.

Black Jack's palms had been greased with enough greenbacks until he was persuaded to come along and finish dealing the game among this motley collection of players. As he began dealing, it was easy to see that Lacy Laci was way out in front of the men. Almost all of the money on the table was in front of her. Her pile of currency would go back and forth, lower and higher, until finally she had it all.

Big Bob Flowers said what all the men playing at the table were thinking, "Dang Laci, how're we supposed to win against you? You're so danged distracting."

She just smiled.

As Lacy Laci was raking in the last of her winnings to her side of the table, the other players were rising to go recuperate from the lashing she gave them at the poker table.

Just then, a familiar face walked up to the table. He had a strikingly beautiful lady at his side.

Big Bob was the first to hold out his hand. "Hello mister lawman. Haven't seen you since Lone Creek."

Dango Durango shook his hand, "Fancy seeing y'all here. I wondered if y'all just left the game where it ended." He gestured to the lady standing beside him. "This is my new bride, Savanna Durango."

The poker players all greeted her.

"We're on our honeymoon."

Savanna added. "I've managed to get him to agree to stay away from hunting the next bounty for a couple of weeks."

She smiled. A glistening glow seemed to shine on her.

Jackson P. interjected, "Dango, it's rumored that you caught that Zulu Outlaw gang."

"It ain't no rumor. They've gone to trial already and each of them was hanged the day after the hearing."

"You don't say. That was mighty quick."

Strychnine Jim exclaimed, "Not fast enough if you ask me. Those were some evil men. That's good, if you ask me that they all hung for their crimes."

"Oh, I misspoke. One of them got away. Ol' Clankie Claster slipped away while they were being herded from the jail to the gallows. They almost caught

up with him, but he evaded capture. No idea where

he is now. The rest of the gang, Zeke Scott, Slim One-Eye, and Copperhead Cooper, are all stone-cold dead."

"Serves 'em right. Just the condition they left the folks in over at Ernie's Trading Square was enough for every single one of them to hang."

Dango replied, "You wouldn't believe it, but every blessed one of them folks recovered completely already."

Lacy Laci almost squealed in delight in her southern dialect, "Are you serious? They all actually improved? How in the world?"

"If I told you, you wouldn't believe it." Dango thought back to a prayer he'd said on the trail to Claster's Caverns.

Lacy Laci continued, "Maybe we can have dinner together later, and you can tell me all about it."

Savanna pulled Dango closer to her and answered before he could, "I don't think so darling."

It wasn't noticeable if Savanna or Dango walked away from the poker players first. But at that very moment while Lacy Laci was still thinking of what to say next, Dango and Savanna turned and walked away, heading to the honeymoon suite of the Creole Princess.

Chapter Thirty

Dango and Savannah had been married just before they came across the poker players on the paddlewheel boat steaming down the Mississippi. The honeymoon was as great as expected.

The wedding had also been spectacular. One note of interest was that it was a double wedding. Dango and Savannah shared the day of their nuptials with Weed and Pricilla. Turnip stood up front proudly as best man for both of them with his firearm ready.

Dango and Savannah sailed the Mississippi, then headed out west back to Colorado, enjoying every minute.

Weed took Pricilla on her dream honeymoon to the Yucatan Peninsula. To her surprise, her parents and sister had been located and were living safely back in their hometown between the Gulf of Mexico and the Mayan Ruins. She visited with several other family members, also.

Ernie and Erline Session continued running the Trading Square. They also became pastors and built a church in Lone Creek. They would tell of how they were miraculously brought back from the throngs of death. They both thought they'd visited Hell and told of mass delirium that existed in that place.

Sheriff CW Lee filled them in later, that they and their customers, that day had been in mass confusion.

That didn't discount the horribleness of an eternal place of torment, but said this only added credence to how great of a deliverance they had experienced.

Dango had heard rumors of Clankie Claster being spotted out near Hangman's Creek, Texas. Savannah would have to kiss him goodbye again soon, knowing he'd be on the hunt in Texas.

Before he left Colorado again for Texas, Dango had the poem he'd read to Savannah during their wedding framed for their home. He named it Savannah.It read:

You're my most precious darling

We'll walk side by side

My heart was yours

When first I saw you

Today you'll be my lovely bride

Hand in hand we'll walk forever

Sweet words I'll whisper in your ear

Savannah, sweetheart how I love you

I will always hold you ever near

One day we shall teach our children

All about God's greatest love

How He brought us together

From His home in Heaven above

My darling we shall forever

Be together every day

Knowing you will always love me

This prayer I'll always pray